Sha'Tanya
UNDERRATED

Sha'Tanya

UNDERRATED

MARIO HERBERT

CONTENTS

Introduction

This is the story of Sha'Tanya Carter, a snarky, hair-gel-abusing teenage girl whose world has been turned upside down.

She's had some intriguing adventures, which have taught her some valuable life lessons, but life lessons often come with painful consequences; she's lost her longest-standing friendships, and was forced to repeat her forth form year with mostly strangers.

These adventures and lessons were chronicled in *Sha'Tanya Unleashed* and *Sha'Tanya Undone*, but it's time for Sha'Tanya to rise from the ashes.

Can Sha'Tanya succeed where she has failed before? Can she exceed the expectations of those who expect her to fail? Can she overcome those who tower over her?

Answers abound in the stories you are about to read, which coincide with events seen and referenced in *Adrian at Loggerheads*. No prior reading is required to thoroughly enjoy that which awaits you, so turn the page and let the adventures begin!

DOGGED DETERMINATION

The shrill cry of a rooster pierced the stillness of the early morning. Sha'Tanya's eyes popped open and started to adjust to the darkness around her. She rose from her resting place on the bottom of a twin-sized bunk bed, and proceeded to stretch, causing her old, off-white nightgown to rise above her midthighs. With her eyes adjusted to the darkness, she grabbed an exercise book from under her pillow and made her way out of the cramped bedroom, leaving behind her mother and two other family members in deep sleep.

She then proceeded to go down a wooden staircase, one metre from her bedroom door, preoccupied with her academic reality. As she reached the middle of the sixteen-step staircase, she could still hear her principal's words echoing in her mind.

"This is the worst your grades have ever been," she remembered the principal saying, "and unfortunately, you will have to repeat your fourth year."

By the time she reached the last step, she remembered the encouragement she had received from a very good school acquaintance, Adrian, who was going into fourth form for the first time.

"Look on the bright side," she remembered him saying, "you already know the syllabus and you already have the notes; you have a head start on the rest of us."

As she exited the staircase and made her way into the combined kitchen and dining room on the right, she mentally prepared herself for an early morning study session before the prevailing peace and quiet could be vanquished by her housemates. Just as she was about to flip the light switch, however, she was startled by the sound of a low growl and a pungent odour.

"What trouble is this?" she thought to herself, as she cautiously raised her hand to the switch with a racing heart.

In short order, the room was inundated with light, causing Sha'Tanya's eyes to readjust themselves. The readjustment brought into focus a big, brown and white, broad-headed dog with blue eyes, beyond the six-seater dining set, in the doorway next to the kitchen counter. As the dog's low growl turned into a deep bark, Sha'Tanya's heart went from racing to throbbing. She started screaming as she took off running with the beast in pursuit.

"Stand down, Hercules!" cried a loud, rough voice from the kitchen.

Sha'Tanya didn't stop running, nor screaming till she was up the stairs, at which time, she looked back to see a tall, dark, muscular, bareback, heavily tattooed man at the foot of the staircase holding the dog by the collar. His hair was cornrowed, his face was harder than a tennis court and his eyes were more piercing than a vaccine. This was her cousin, Raymond, who had moved into a makeshift hut in the back yard, bringing his four pit bull terriers with him—Hercules, Titan, Sinbad and Goliath.

As Sha'Tanya stood at the top of the stairs, catching her breath, she realised that the entire house was now awake. Her slim, dark, red-haired, nightgown-clad mother exited her bedroom, on her right, along with her two younger, pyjama-clad cousins, Christopher and Zachary. Four adult, female cousins exited the room next door to her own, clad in nightgowns, and the door to her immediate left opened to reveal a bareback uncle. Two aunts and her dark, greyed grandmother, all in their nightgowns, soon appeared behind her uncle. Finally, another bareback uncle appeared at the bottom of the staircase, next to Raymond; this was Jimmy, a freelance mechanic who slept on the living room couch.

"What's with all this screaming at this ungodly hour!" cried Sha'Tanya's grandmother as the other family members stared intently.

"I went downstairs to study and a whole dog was in the house, growling at me," cried Sha'Tanya, passionately, "a … whole … dog!"

"Relax yourself, lil' girl," said Raymond, dismissively, "Hercules was trying to play with you, and you behaved foolish."

"Play with me?" cried Sha'Tanya, arms akimbo

with wide eyes. "Error—he's a pit bull, trained for fighting!"

"Listen, girl, go back in your bed and let there be less noise in here," cried one of her cousins from the room next door to her own, "it's too early for this foolishness!"

"You shouldn't even be up at this hour," cried another relative, "talking ign'rance 'bout studying; school ain't even starting till next week."

"I ain't supposed to be studying?" cried Sha'Tanya, with attitude and a quizzical look. "But he's supposed to bring pit bulls in here with people's children?"

"Everybody in this house had to repeat a year; you ain't special," cried another relative, "get over it and sleep till the correct time; you wouldn't have to worry 'bout dogs."

Sha'Tanya was inundated with a flood of emotions. She was angry with her cousin, Raymond, for endangering her life, and she was hurt by the reactions from her family members. Their comments reverberated in her mind, all congealed together. She wasn't conscious of who had said what, but she felt thoroughly belittled, powerless and woefully insignificant.

"Drop it and come back to bed," whispered her mother, before she could verbalise her emotions.

As she went back to her room and the crowd dispersed, she never imagined she could feel so alone in an overcrowded house.

Eventually, the rest of the household started their day, but Sha'Tanya had no interest in mingling with them. She waited until she figured most of them had left for work, before making her way down the stairs again. To her relief, her uncle, Jimmy, had left to fix a vehicle, her unemployed cousin, Raymond, had apparently left the premises, and her two younger cousins had been taken to spend the day with another relative; it was just her and her grandmother.

She basked in the peace and quiet, as she entered the kitchen and dining area once again. On the left side of the room was a small, four burner stove, a small fridge and a single L-shaped counter with a toaster oven and a sink, set over cupboards. Next to this counter was a metal door with a louver, leading into the back yard. With the kitchen counter and appliances, there was just enough space left in the room to hold a wrought iron, six-seater dining set. Behind the table, on the right side of the room, was another door, leading to a small bathroom.

Sha'Tanya made her way to the counter and mixed flour, sugar, water and some spices together to make a thick batter. She then moved over to the stove, heated a frying pan with some oil, poured the mixture into the pan in discrete discs, and fried them until they were brown on each side; she had created a Barbadian budget breakfast dish—bakes.

While the pan was still hot, she retrieved an egg from the fridge and proceeded to crack it into a bowl. As the egg shell was cracked on the side of the bowl, some of the egg got on her nightgown.

"This is the only nightgown I have, and now it smells like egg," she thought to herself, before verbalising that thought in a single word.

"Error!"

She promptly turned off the stove, dashed into the small bathroom, pulled off the nightgown and put it to soak in a small ceramic sink which she had filled with soapy water.

"It's a good thing it's only me and my grandmother in the house," she thought, as she dashed out of the bathroom and up the stairs to find alternative clothing.

In a few minutes, she was dashing down the stairs again in a short, yellow shirt, a short blue pants and a pair of flat shoes. She returned to the bathroom and rinsed the nightgown until she felt satisfied the egg had been exorcised from the fabric. With her garment sanitised, she wrang it as dry as she could, exited the bathroom into the dining area, and carried it through the back door into the doggy back yard.

The backyard was fully concreted and enclosed by a tall, galvanised fence. Along the perimeter of that fence was a makeshift, plywood hut with a single window and door, and four wooden dog cages with names—Hercules, Titan, Sinbad and Goliath. Stretched across the middle of the yard were several clotheslines.

Sha'Tanya made her way to the clotheslines and affixed her sanitised nightgown to the line with clothespins which were already on the line. As she affixed the final clothespin, she saw something highly disturbing in her peripheral vision. She tuned her gaze to investigate, and made a startling discovery; the cage labelled "Goliath" was wide open.

"No, no, no, no," she thought, as she cautiously

stepped backwards—in the direction of the kitchen door—with a pounding heart. As she reversed her steps, she visually surveyed the yard, looking for the beast.

"Maybe Raymond took him out for a walk," she thought, trying to reassure herself as she continued to step backwards, "I might be panicking for nothing."

Suddenly, an enormous, broad-headed, chocolate-brown dog with dark brown eyes, emerged from the side of the hut, and immediately started to growl.

"Be cool, be cool," she thought to herself, but her heart did not cooperate with her brain, and she turned and took flight towards the door.

As she reached the door, she glanced behind her to see the dog right on her heels, sending her heart into overdrive. She didn't try to close the door as she dashed through it; the beast was too close on her heels. She barrelled through the kitchen in an adrenaline-fuelled frenzy, throwing down one of the dining chairs as she dashed past it, in hopes of slowing the advance of the beast. She was too winded to scream as she ascended multiple stairs at a time, unsure how she was accomplishing the feat.

As she reached the top of the staircase, she glanced behind her to see the beast ascending, its paws hitting the wooden steps with the force of two small humans. She dared not try to make it to her own bedroom, but dashed through the nearest door, on her right, into her uncle's makeshift bedroom.

The room, created by a plywood partition near the entrance of Sha'Tanya's grandmother's bedroom, was barely bigger than the twin-sized bed it contained.

There was a wooden dowel rod, reminiscent of a broomstick, stretched across one side of the makeshift room for the hanging of clothes. In the plywood partition was a door, leading into the original bedroom.

Sha'Tanya dashed past her uncle's bed and through the door in the partition, into her grandmother's bedroom. Once through, she turned and slammed the door shut as the beast approached it.

As she tried to catch her breath, she could hear the dog barking and trying to push the door open; she could also smell it through the door. As soon as she had locked the door, she was startled by shrill screaming from behind her. She turned to see her grandmother sitting up in her queen-sized bed, between two nightstands, screaming at the top of her aged lungs.

"Look a' my lot; a robber come for me," she screamed. "Murder, murder, murder!"

"What trouble is this, now?" Sha'Tanya thought, before addressing her grandmother's error—literally.

"Error!" cried Sha'Tanya, arms akimbo. "You telling me you ain't know your own granddaughter?"

Before she could explain the situation, her grandmother had exited the bed and was pulling a chamber pot, half-filled with urine, from under the bed.

"Where you think you going with that pee?" cried Sha'Tanya.

"This old girl ain't going down so easy," cried the grandmother, as she secured the chamber pot and lifted it in Sha'Tanya's direction, "I' been saving this up just for vagabonds like you!"

"This old woman's head screwed on backwards?"

Sha'Tanya thought, in alarm, as her grandmother proceeded to throw the contents of the chamber pot at her.

"What the bird!" she cried, as she narrowly jumped out of the path of the urine, and landed on the floor on the other side of the bed.

"Granny, it's Sha'Tanya!" she screamed, as she cautiously rose from the floor with her hands outstretched in a defensive posture. "Sha'Tanya, Sha'Tanya, Sha'Tanya!"

"Wait, I ain't realise that's you; I thought it was a robber," cried the old lady, alternating her gaze between Sha'Tanya and the chamber pot. "That's good pee gone to waste; now I gotta fill back this chamber pot in case a real robber comes."

"Error," cried Sha'Tanya, in an exasperated tone, "the robbers ain't looking for houses like this; they want people with money."

Granny returned the chamber pot to its original position, under the bed, as Sha'Tanya explained the situation with the dog, which could still be heard nearby.

"Well, you might as well relax yourself and look through the window for Raymond," said Granny in an indifferent tone, after hearing the situation.

"I have to wait in this frowsy room until whenever he decides to show up, before I can eat my breakfast, bathe, refresh my rusty hair gel and study?" thought Sha'Tanya, glancing at the urine on the floor before verbalizing the thought in a single word.

"Error!" she cried, arms akimbo. "You gotta do something 'bout Raymond and these dogs!"

"Not me!" cried Granny, promptly. "That boy' head ain't good!"

It was at this time Sha'Tanya realised that the adults in the house were afraid of Raymond. That powerless feeling she had felt earlier that morning was back, and it was amplified. She hated the fact that she couldn't change her situation, and she hated the fact that the people with the ability to change it, were too afraid to do so.

"This 'fambily' settles for anything," she thought, as she looked through one of two windows, peering at the road in front of the house, in hopes of seeing Raymond's tennis-court face. "They settle for failure, poor grades and unfair treatment; I ain't settling for this situation."

Sha'Tanya turned around with determination, and surveyed the room.

"Granny, I need to borrow a bed sheet," she said, with a gleam in her eyes, "maybe two."

Minutes later, she had fashioned a long rope from bedsheets, with various knots tied into it for easier grip when climbing. She tied one end of the makeshift rope around the middle beam of one of the casement windows in the room, and threw the other end out the window.

"If you drop off that sheet," started Granny, as Sha'Tanya pushed one leg through the window, backwards, "don't look for me to carry you to the 'horsepital'!"

"Believe me, the 'horsepital' would be better than being trapped in this frowsy room," Sha'Tanya replied, as she put the other foot through the window, repeating her grandmother's mispronunciation of the word 'hospital'.

With both legs through the window, she held on to the window sill and lowered her body through the window. She then took hold of the knots she had made, and climbed down to the small, concreted, open front yard below.

As she climbed, she was so focused on being careful, that she didn't even hear the engine of a car behind her. Finally, on the concreted ground, she breathed a sigh of relief, which was quickly vanquished by the brief, piercing sound of a siren.

Sha'Tanya spun around quickly, to see a police car in the street outside the house, with two officers in the front, staring intently at her. The driver was a short, clear man with a low haircut, and next to him was a dark woman, with a short hairstyle. Sha'Tanya could see from the way these officers were staring at her, that they had the wrong idea.

"What trouble is this, now?" she thought, totally exasperated from the hardships endured already for that morning.

"This ain't what it looks like, officers," she cried, as the sheet rope was pulled back up through the window behind her, "I live here!"

"Right," said the female officer, as she exited the car, "I'm sure you do."

"I ain't carrying anything on me," she cried, passionately, as the officer closed the car door behind her, "you can see that I ain't stealing anything!"

"Your hands might be empty," started the officer, as she stepped slowly towards Sha'Tanya's position, "but a strip search might reveal some very interesting things."

"This woman intoxicated? Nobody ain't stripping me!" thought Sha'Tanya, with a throbbing heart, before verbalising her thoughts in a single word.

"Error!" she cried, holding her hands out in front of her, gesturing to the officer to halt. "I tell you I live here!"

"Prove it in sixty seconds or you're getting in this car," said the officer, with a stern face and folded arms.

Sha'Tanya turned and started shouting for her grandmother, being sure to keep the officer in view at all times. To her dismay, the old woman did not appear.

"What to do, what to do?" she thought, as anxiety burned in her stomach and her heart raced like an Olympic sprinter. Her immediate neighbours were all at work, her grandmother had possibly forgotten who she was, and she couldn't open the front door because the dog was loose.

To Sha'Tanya's dismay, the officer unfolded her arms and resumed her approach. Sha'Tanya wasn't keen on trying to explain the dog situation, but she knew she had to do something, so she did; she ran like the wind.

As she ran towards the end of her apartment block, the female officer was in hot pursuit on foot, and the sound of the siren told her that the car was mobile once again.

"I can't outrun a car," she thought, as she ran, "I need to get off the road."

She could hear the female officer reporting into her radio, "Officer Rice, badge number '1121' … in pursuit of a suspected robber … teenager, female, dark, average height … possible accomplice inside house …"

This was all too much for Sha'Tanya, and she zoned out the officers completely and directed all of her physical and mental faculties to fleeing. She dashed around the end of the block, and the car turned onto the road next to her, but she didn't stay on that path; she dashed through a narrow alley between the back yards of her apartment block, and the block in the adjacent street. As she ran through the alley, with continuous, tall galvanised fences on either side, she fixed her gaze on the street she could see in the distance, at the end of the alley. She was almost there, and was intent that her feet would not fail her in her moment of despair. As she approached the light at the end of the tunnel, the police car suddenly appeared at the end of that tunnel, sending her into a panic. In that moment, as she approached the car, which was blocking the exit of the alley, she could hear the female officer's words echoing in her mind.

"A strip search might reveal some very interesting things."

Despite the arrival of the car, she was more determined than ever to escape; she could not allow herself to be taken into custody and searched in such a manner.

Finally, she reached the end of the alley, fuelled by

concentrated adrenaline and fear, which propelled her into the air. She landed on the bonnet of the car and rolled her body over it, to land in the road on the other side of the car. Unfortunately, by the time she picked herself up from the ground, the driver had exited the car and his partner had caught up to her. Before she could process what was happening, a firm hand gripped her by the arm and a small group of onlookers from surrounding blocks were forming a small crowd nearby.

Just as tears of shame and despair prepared to invade her eyes, a tall, dark, muscular, hard-faced man with piercing eyes emerged out of the crowd and approached the police car—her cousin, Raymond, in a sleeveless shirt, revealing his heavily tattooed arms. Sha'Tanya never thought she could be so happy to see that tennis-court face, but in that moment, the source of her peril had temporarily become the source of her salvation.

In short order, the misunderstanding was cleared up with the police officers and Raymond was brought up-to-date on the Goliath incident.

"Glad to get that cleared up, that woman was talking 'bout strip searching me!" said Sha'Tanya, with a sigh of relief as the officers drove away and the crowd dispersed. "I just want to get home and start my day."

"I ain't ready to go back home yet," said Raymond, indifferently, "I gotta finalise some things for the fight this morning."

"We just live 'round the corner!" cried Sha'Tanya, in a voice of despair. "I ain't eat for the morning, I ain't even bathe; I just want to put myself right and do some studying."

DOGGED DETERMINATION

"You gotta stop getting hot and sweaty over things you can't change!" cried Raymond, emphatically, as he shook his index finger at Sha'Tanya. "I run things and I call the shots; the sooner you accept that, life would be simpler for you!"

Sha'Tanya just held her head down in total defeat. She had resolved not to settle for her situation like the rest of her family, but after all she had been through to find Raymond, she had failed to change anything in her favour.

"Get to know the dogs, place some bets at the fights," Raymond continued, as he led her away, "your mother ain't gotta know 'bout it."

Sha'Tanya had no desire to know the dogs, and she definitely had no desire to get wrapped up in Raymond's world of dog fighting, but it seemed evident that it would be much simpler to work with him than against him. Everyone else in the house had clearly reached that resolve, and she thought maybe it was time for her to do the same and find ways to coexist with him and the dogs.

Thirty minutes later, after meeting with several of Raymond's friends and checking out the venue for the fight, Sha'Tanya finally made it back to the house. Raymond entered first, secured the dog and then signalled for her to enter. She immediately made her way upstairs to let her grandmother know the coast was clear, and to grab a towel and some clothes from her bedroom. She then made her way to the kitchen, put her bakes in the toaster oven, and entered the shower while her bakes were reheated on a timer.

As she showered, she looked around her at the myriad of undergarments hung over the top of the shower curtain, around the shower head and shower faucet. This was something that had greatly annoyed her when she moved into her grandmother's residence, but she had since learned to live with it. As she washed the day-old gel out of her hair, she pondered the prospect of learning to live with Raymond and the dogs.

Minutes later, she exited the bathroom, dressed again, with her towel around her head. She retrieved her bakes from the toaster oven, and made her way to the back door. She opened the louver and saw Raymond in the yard looking at the cages.

"Trying to decide which one to take to the fight?" she asked, in a loud voice.

"Come," Raymond cried, turning and signalling to her, "coast clear!"

She opened the door and entered the yard, bakes in hand, still surveying the cages and satisfying herself that the coast was, indeed, clear.

"Glad to see you taking an interest," said Raymond, as Sha'Tanya stood next to him, eating her bakes. "Which one you think I should take?"

"Goliath," she replied, promptly, in a matter-of-fact way, "he's the biggest."

"Error," said Raymond, calmly, with a grin, "Goliath may be the biggest, but he ain't as vicious and determined as Sinbad."

"Really?" replied Sha'Tanya, with a sceptical look.

"You may be more afraid of Hercules and Goliath because of their size, but winning a fight ain't always 'bout size or power," said Raymond, looking at Sha'Tanya with his piercing eyes. "It's all 'bout determination."

"Interesting," said Sha'Tanya, genuinely intrigued as she looked at the smaller dog through the meshed door of the cage.

"So, you coming to the fight?" asked Raymond, with a grin. "I' just about ready to move."

"I ain't so sure 'bout that one," Sha'Tanya promptly replied, holding up one hand in a defensive posture while the other held the plate.

"I ain't rescue you from the police earlier?" asked Raymond. "I ain't gonna let anything happen to you—real talk."

"Alright," said Sha'Tanya, after taking a moment to ponder intently, "but not with my hair like this, and not in these clothes; I will meet you there in a few minutes."

Sha'Tanya left Raymond in the yard, shaking his head, and returned to the house to get herself ready.

Fifteen minutes later, she was stepping through the front door in a fuchsia pink shirt, a short denim pants and a pair of fuchsia pink flat shoes. Her hair was freshly gelled to her head and glistened beautifully. Her neck was inundated with baby powder and her lips were glossed.

"Sha'Tanya Carter is unleashed," she thought, as she left the house and started for the venue of the fight.

Minutes later, she was approaching a grove which housed an informal vehicle scrapyard amongst the trees. The scrapyard was operated by a resident of a nearby apartment block, who had numerous wrecked cars distributed throughout the grove in no particular order. In the middle of the grove, however, there was some order; there were four derelict cars positioned in a square, forming an arena approximately five metres square, with two small openings opposite each other. There were concrete blocks lining the inside of the arena, making it impossible to enter or exit the arena from under the four enclosing vehicles.

When Sha'Tanya arrived, there was already a crowd assembled around the arena, in the shade of the trees. As she made her way closer to the arena, she saw Raymond and another muscular, dark man, holding their dogs just outside the opposing entrances to the area.

Raymond had, indeed, chosen Sinbad to fight. Sinbad was a reddish-brown beast, with hazel-coloured eyes. He wasn't as big as Hercules but he was still muscular and fierce-looking in his own right. The opposing beast was bigger, with a chocolate-coloured coat and dark brown eyes.

Sha'Tanya made eye contact with Raymond, who gave her a nod, just before a tall, clear, bareback man, who was apparently the referee, gave a hand signal and the furious dogs were released into the arena. The crowd cheered as the dogs started wrestling, each trying to get a bite hold on the other. Sha'Tanya was afraid to look; she didn't care for Sinbad, but that didn't mean she wanted to see him—or any other dog—torn to shreds for entertainment and personal gain.

Suddenly, as if in response to her aversion to seeing

the fight continue, the cheering was shattered by the piercing sound of a bullhorn.

"Do not move," shouted an artificially amplified voice, "you are surrounded!"

Panic ensued as police officers rushed into the grove from all angles, accompanied by other officials, who Sha'Tanya figured were animal control officers. She wasted no time in fleeing the scene. She didn't look around her to see who else was fleeing, or who was being apprehended.

"I should have stayed in the house and studied," she thought, as she approached the boundary of the grove, "I ain't cut out for all of this running—not in the space of one morning."

In short order, she cleared the grove, to be greeted by two armed officers, instructing her to halt—the same two officers who had chased her earlier that morning.

A few minutes later, she was being led to a police car in handcuffs, along with several other people. As she reached the car, she heard a familiar voice addressing the officers who were carrying her.

"Officers, that's my lil' cousin," came Raymond's voice, from inside the police car, "she ain't involved in this."

"It's an offense to be a spectator at an illegal dog fight," said the female officer, coldly.

"Officer, she's a good girl, she ain't studying these things," cried Raymond, passionately. "It's me that made her come down here; all she was interested in was school work—she's a good girl."

Sha'Tanya was shocked at her cousin's selfless defence of her. He had promised her that he wouldn't let anything happen to her, and it appeared he was trying to live up to that promise. It appeared that he did have some sense of care for her, or at a minimum, some sense of honouring his word. This revelation notwithstanding, Sha'Tanya felt no compassion for her cousin's demise.

"Fine, the girl can go," said the officer, finally, "but not before I give her a good talking to."

The officer proceeded to release Sha'Tanya's handcuffs, then led her several metres away from the vehicle before addressing her.

"We got off to a rocky start … but it's been a pleasure doing business with you, young lady," said the officer to Sha'Tanya, as they both backed the police car, several metres behind them. "The four-legged dogs have been apprehended by the animal control unit, and we have apprehended the two-legged variety."

"I didn't think you would get here in such a short space of time," said Sha'Tanya.

"It was tight but we had officers patrolling nearby districts, and an animal control team had just made a house call in this area," said the officer, to which Sha'Tanya just nodded.

"You've clearly memorised my name and badge number; feel free to contact me again if you've stumbled onto anything else major," continued the officer. "You're clearly a very brave and confident young lady."

"I don't feel that way lately," said Sha'Tanya, finally breaking her silence, "but I learned a valuable lesson today; winning a fight ain't always 'bout size or power, but determination."

The officer gave her a nod and signalled her to go.

"Don't let me hear 'bout you in any more trouble!" shouted the officer, sternly, as Sha'Tanya ran away, hearing Raymond's words echoing in her mind.

"I run things and I call the shots; the sooner you accept that, life would be simpler for you!"

She vanquished the echo as she uttered a single word.

"Error."

SHA'TANYA ENTERPRISES

The wind gently blew a falling leaf past Sha'Tanya's glistening, excessively gelled hair, as she sat on a bench in the shade of a big tree in the school yard. She hardly noticed the leaf as it passed her face, as she was in deep concentration, turning the pages of an exercise book. She was so engrossed in the book that she didn't notice a slim, dark boy approaching her until he addressed her.

"Sha'Tanya Carter, at school early!" cried the boy, in a loud voice, causing her head to pop up from the book. "Wonders never cease."

It was her new classmate and friend, Adrian Manning. She had been on a disastrous date with him a year prior, when he was still a junior. Since that time, he had remained a cordial acquaintance, but now, she was repeating her fourth year and she considered him a good friend; he was the only person in her new class she really knew, and he was the only person who stuck with her throughout her emotional transition.

"Don't be calling out my whole name, Adrian," replied Sha'Tanya, giving him a narrow stare as he approached, "we ain't on a full-name basis—not just yet."

"The excessive hair gel and close-fitting uniform indicate that you are Sha'Tanya—but you are at school early," started Adrian, pulling his chin with a quizzical stare as he sat himself down next to her. "Come clean; admit you are an imposter from a parallel universe, posing as the real Sha'Tanya."

"Something wrong with your head," replied Sha'Tanya, laughing heartily. "Look, it's just easier for me to study at school than in my house; my 'fambily' ain't care 'bout studying and they don't make it easy."

"What kind of family doesn't care about studying?" asked Adrian, with discombobulation etched upon his face.

"The kind of 'fambily' where everybody had to re-peat a year and nobody left school with much certifi-cates," started Sha'Tanya, with attitude, "so they ain't expecting me to do any better—but that is a' error on their part!"

"That settles it; you are a different Sha'Tanya, from an alternate universe," cried Adrian, with a chuckle, "but I like this Sha'Tanya; choosing to study instead of waiting around for the reckless, hype bus."

"Error!" cried Sha'Tanya, promptly, raising one hand in a defensive posture. "I left home early enough to catch *Turbulence* on the early trip; it wasn't as hype as the late trip, but still way better than riding in one of those boring, musty, rust-bucket buses."

"I was mistaken; you are definitely the Sha'Tanya I know," said Adrian, executing a facepalm as Sha'Tanya stared at him intently. "What are you studying?"

"History," started Sha'Tanya, returning her attention to the exercise book. "Trying to brush up on Christopher Columbus; I think he's the man that discovered the Great Wall of China—or something like that."

Adrian rose to his feet, holding his head, then turned to Sha'Tanya, arms akimbo, with wide eyes.

"What?" asked Sha'Tanya, quizzically.

"Let me put this in terms you will understand," cried Adrian, staring at her intently with wide eyes. "Error!"

"I might be just fooling myself," said Sha'Tanya, with a sigh, as she held her head down, feeling a bit ashamed, "I might be destined to be 'dumpsy' like all my other 'fambily' members."

"Don't even go there; you are not duncy, "started Adrian, firmly but tenderly, as he sat and put one arm around her shoulder. "You're on a good path; you may just need to get a little help."

"You mean, like, extra lessons?" she asked, holding her head up and looking across at Adrian.

"Yeah, why not?" cried Adrian, making a quizzical gesture with his free hand.

"My 'fambily' ain't care 'bout lessons; I would have to raise the money myself," cried Sha'Tanya, giving Adrian a deadpan stare. "You going to help me figure out how to raise this money?"

"I would love to," started Adrian, rising from his seat and making eye contact with Sha'Tanya, "but right now, I'm orchestrating a scheme to get rid of the abusive, new P.E. teacher, and that's taking up all my brain power."

"You and your adventurous life," replied Sha'Tanya, shaking her head with a wide smile, "I hope for your sake this scheme ends better than your last one."

"You just had to remind me about my suspension," Adrian moaned. "Don't jinx it; Mr. Cumberbatch will be gone in short order, and then I can help you with your issue."

"Don't worry, I got this," cried Sha'Tanya, with attitude, "you ain't the only one that can come up with schemes."

Sha'Tanya looked on admiringly as Adrian walked away. After being disowned by her former best friend, Laurel, Adrian had proven himself to be a decent friend to her. She admired his intelligence and witty mind, but in that moment, she challenged herself to come up with a solution to her problem without his assistance.

Later that morning, Sha'Tanya was sitting next to Adrian, in her classroom at the first of six desks, in the first of four rows. She was still trying to think of a way to earn some money for lessons. Her thought process was truncated, as a short, stocky, spectacled teacher entered the class and stood behind the teacher's desk, which was centrally positioned at the top of the off-white room, under a huge whiteboard; this was Mrs. Gibbs-Sealy.

"We are congregated here once again to perfect our mastery of the gloriously nuanced English language," she started, in a high-pitched, enthusiastic voice. "Each desk should now be furnished with an exercise book, your homework and some manner of writing implement."

The students complied with the directive and Mrs. Gibbs-Sealy started to move around the class, collecting homework assignments.

"Akanni Johnson, where is my homework?" cried the teacher, as she reached a dark, thick-lipped Rastafarian of average height and build, sitting in the middle of the back row. "Surrender the assignment forthwith!"

"If it's your homework," started Akanni, in a smug tone, "shouldn't you know where it is?"

The class snickered as Mrs. Gibbs-Sealy turned red and stared intently at Akanni.

"You have exercised your mouth inappropriately," cried the teacher, in her shrill voice, "therefore, you will exercise your hand in the repeated scripting of a correctional statement!"

"Huh?" said Akanni, with a dumbfounded look on his face. "Pardon me."

"You will write lines!" screamed the teacher, as the class collectively chuckled. "This is what you will write—twenty-five times!"

Akanni scrambled to open his book and get his pen in hand before the teacher began to dictate.

"I must behave myself," started the teacher.

"Got it," cried Akanni, with a grin.

"I am not finished!" cried the teacher, before continuing to dictate the line to be written. "Good behaviour is so old, that there is no record of when it was invented …"

Akanni's grin disappeared as the teacher continued and his classmates looked on with shock and amusement etched upon their faces.

"Surely, if ancient people, with less education and knowledge of the world, can figure out how to behave properly," continued the teacher, "so can I, in the early twenty-first century."

The class openly snickered as the teacher concluded her dictation. A visibly bewildered Akanni did, in fact, surrender an assignment to her, and the class continued. Sha'Tanya wasn't as amused as the other students seemed to be; her mind was going.

At the end of the period, Sha'Tanya promptly approached Akanni at the back of the class.

"So, 'bout these lines you gotta write," she started, before being promptly interrupted.

"If you're here to laugh at me," started Akanni, aggressively, "I ain't got time for you and that; I have a lot of lines to write!"

"I know," said Sha'Tanya, with a ponderous look, "one 'line' is actually … six lines in an exercise book?"

"Try seven!" cried Akanni, with a stern look.

"I would hate to have to write all those lines," said Sha'Tanya, with a ponderous look, "unless, of course, somebody was paying me to write them."

"Seriously," cried Akanni, in an excited tone, "you would write lines for somebody else?"

"If the price was right," replied Sha'Tanya, with a grin.

"I can give you twenty-five cents a page."

"Error!" cried Sha'Tanya. "A dollar a page."

"Ridiculous!" cried Akanni, with a disdainful stare. "Fifty cents a page."

"Done!" said Sha'Tanya, with a smile.

By that time, the teacher for the next class was arriving, and Akanni surrendered the book to Sha'Tanya, who promptly returned to her seat.

By utilising short moments of downtime between classes, by the time the bell rang for recess, she had already analysed his handwriting, and written a couple of pages.

As she rose to go to the canteen, she overheard a short, clear boy with wavy hair, lamenting the idea of joining a line in the canteen.

"I can't believe I gotta go in that canteen," cried the boy, "and fight the crowd to get food that ain't even taste good."

"You know, Allain," started Sha'Tanya, as she approached the boy, "I could fight the crowd for you; you could just sit here and wait till I deliver the lunch."

"Really?" cried Allain, excitedly.

"If the price was right," replied Sha'Tanya, with a grin.

"I can give you fifty cents."

"Error!" cried Sha'Tanya. "Two dollars."

"Ridiculous—you gotta go in the line anyway," cried Allain, with a disdainful stare. "One dollar—final offer."

"Done!" said Sha'Tanya, with a smile.

"I want in on this, too," cried a slim, clear-skinned girl named Kerrie, with braces and corn-rowed hair; Sha'Tanya had gained another client.

SHA'TANYA UNDERRATED

By the end of the day, Sha'Tanya had made six dollars; she had earned two dollars by delivering lunch to Allain and Kerrie, and Akanni's punishment amounted to one hundred and seventy-five lines, requiring eight pages for a four-dollar pay-out. She had also received an overnight job to write lines for a popular girl in the class, named Richelle, and attracted interest from other students for lunch duty.

Sha'Tanya's confidence in her ability to enterprise was greatly bolstered, birthing yet another idea to increase her disposable income. She got up early the next morning to make bakes—a popular Barbadian breakfast dish—but she hid some of them in her backpack so she could have them for lunch, while still receiving money for lunch.

That day, she had increased her canteen service clients from two to four, all at the same rate of one dollar. With greater confidence in her negotiation skills, however, she decided to negotiate further, and they agreed to pay her two dollars each if she could get their lunches in ten minutes. This proved to be an easy feat, as she was accustomed dealing with disorderly crowds every weekday when she travelled on the hype bus. She managed to return with the lunches in nine minutes, doubling her earnings.

With her job completed, and having exceeded the previous day's earnings, she retrieved her bakes from her backpack and sat at her desk to relax and devour them. As she started to eat, she attracted the attention of a bony, pale white boy, resembling a whitewashed stick insect—Jerome Atkins.

"What are those?" he asked, as she lifted the first of the flat, brown, elliptical discs to her mouth.

"Seriously," started Sha'Tanya, with a deadpan stare, "you never had bakes before?"

"Never heard of them; my maid has never made them," replied Jerome, with an inquisitive expression. "I'm guessing you bake them."

"Error; you fry bakes," said Sha'Tanya, "it's like a pancake but smaller and heavier; don't ask me why we call them bakes."

"Can I taste one?" asked Jerome, with a greedy look on his face.

"This boy's swimming in money, and looking to rob me of the little breakfast I'm trying to eat for lunch," Sha'Tanya thought, but she was in such a good mood after her earnings, that she graciously offered him one of the bakes.

"Wow, this is excellent!" cried Jerome after tasting the bake. "I'll give you five dollars for those bakes, and if you can get them on a regular basis, they're more five-dollar bills with your name on them."

Sha'Tanya liked the sound of this, but she was rather hungry. At that moment, Adrian entered the class with a lunch container in his hand, and Sha'Tanya's mind kicked into gear.

"Done!" she cried, promptly surrendering the bakes to Jerome and receiving her payment as Adrian sat at his desk.

With her newest payment secured, she pulled her chair right next to Adrian's and took a seat.

"So, friend," she started, with a seductive smile,

as she secured the money in a small, padlocked compartment of her backpack, "you going to eat all of that food?"

"Wait a minute," said Adrian, in a critical tone with folded arms, "we ain't on a full-name basis, but you want to be on a half-lunch basis?"

"It was your idea for me to get some extra lessons," cried Sha'Tanya, with attitude and one arm akimbo, "if you can't afford to support my new fundraising business, the least you could do is help me save some money."

"Fine," Adrian replied, in a mildly annoyed tone, "we can share lunch but don't get too cosy; the last thing I need is for people to think I'm falling for you."

"Nobody would fault you; I am dynamite!"

"Get over yourself," replied Adrian, with a smile, as he opened the lunch container, "if this food tasted better, you wouldn't be getting any."

As they prepared to partake of the food, a slim, clear, shapely girl, with excessively gelled hair, entered the classroom and struck a pose in front of Sha'Tanya; this was Richelle, a popular girl, not just in that class, but in that year group.

"Girl, those lines saved my life; the handwriting was matched perfectly," cried Richelle, with attitude. "I gotta pay more attention to you; you seem to be a smart girl!"

"See?" Sha'Tanya whispered to Adrian, as Richelle strutted away. "I ain't the only one that thinks I'm dynamite."

Adrian just grunted but Sha'Tanya felt empowered. By the end of the day, she had made eight dollars from canteen duty, five dollars from Jerome, two dollars and fifty cents from Richelle for overnight writing of lines, and an additional two dollars and fifty cents from Akanni for lines written after recess. She had also been able to save her lunch money, bringing her total income for that day to twenty-three dollars.

The next day, Sha'Tanya was still feeling empowered. That day, by lunch time, Sha'Tanya had already replicated the previous day's earnings, but as she sat, sharing Adrian's lunch, her mind was still fixed on ways she could possibly earn more.

A number of students were in the classroom at that time, and a discussion started up about the upcoming period.

"Listen up—Mrs. Gibbs-Sealy should have marked the homework assignment by now," said Allain, in a loud voice as he sat on the teacher's desk and addressed the room, "you all think you passed?"

"Well, I'm not fooling myself," started Jerome, from his seat in the middle of the class, "I know I got zero; my maid did a horrible job on that assignment."

The students collectively facepalmed themselves.

"I think the real question is whether or not Akanni passed the assignment," started Adrian, in a firm, loud voice, as he turned around to give Akanni—who was in the middle of the back row—a nasty look. "After that stunt he pulled, I think he expected to fail!"

"Yeah, come to think of it, I think he's a likely candidate to fail," said Allain, with a ponderous look on his face.

"Hello," cried Akanni, sternly, "I'm right here!"

"If I was handing in an assignment, and I thought I might pass," continued Allain, ignoring Akanni's outburst, "I would never try to upset the teacher that's marking my work; Akanni definitely failed—and he knows he failed."

Sha'Tanya looked on with intrigue as more students joined the debate.

"I don't know," started Kerrie, from a seat on the left side of the teacher's desk, "these class-clown types like to act stupid in front of the class and then do their work behind the scenes; I think Akanni passed."

"I don't agree," cried Richelle, as she sat in a window sill on the left side of the room, "I think all the class-clown antics just there to hide the fact that these children are stupid; Akanni ain't just fail, he probably got close to zero!"

"Hello," cried Akanni, in a loud voice, "I … am … right … here!"

"Well, I sure hope he gets zero," cried Jerome, excitedly, "it gets lonely at the bottom!"

"Listen up, people, we could make this interesting; I can make a pool," cried Sha'Tanya, jumping up from her seat with a gleam in her eyes, thinking about how Mrs. Gibbs-Sealy liked to publicly announce scores, "two dollars to enter; guess the score on Akanni's assignment, and whoever makes the closest guess, gets the money—minus a ten percent commission for the organiser!"

"Hmm," said Allain, giving Sha'Tanya a critical stare, before speaking further. "Sounds reasonable—count me in!

"I want piece of this action!" cried Richelle, as Akanni rose and proceeded to storm out of the classroom.

"I don't need the money," said Jerome, with a ponderous look, ignoring Akanni's abrupt exit, "but this sounds like fun, so I'm in."

"Alright," said Kerrie, in a soft voice, after taking a moment to ponder, "put me in the pool, too."

Sha'Tanya was pleased that the students had bought into the pool idea, but she also saw a greater opportunity for profit.

"That's seven dollars somebody could make," she said, as the students surrendered their money and wrote their names and predicted scores on a sheet of paper, "and the more people you can get to join the pool, the bigger the pay-out!"

"I like how you think; you're a smart girl," cried Richelle, as she surrendered her money to Sha'Tanya, "I could see this being the next big thing in the school!"

With the money collected, Sha'Tanya removed a padlock from a small compartment of her backpack and pushed the money inside. Allain, Richelle and Kerrie then raced out of the classroom to find more interested parties to join the pool, leaving Sha'Tanya alone with Adrian and Jerome.

"So, you in this pool or not," Sha'Tanya asked, as she sat next to Adrian again.

"Negative," started Adrian, "this is a bad idea."

"Not according to the sixty dollars in this compartment," replied Sha'Tanya, in an indifferent tone, as she fastened the zip on the compartment of the backpack which held the money.

"Look, you're obviously as good at business as I am at schemes, but take it from somebody that just had a great scheme backfire on him," said Adrian, folding his arms, "you have to know where to draw the line; I think you should be contented with what you have."

"Be cool; I got this," said Sha'Tanya, putting the padlock in her pocket in anticipation of more students joining the pool. "Business can only go up from here."

Before their conversation could go any further, Allain was rushing into the classroom with three students desirous of joining the pool. By the time Sha'Tanya had signed them up, Kerrie was arriving with three more students. Before Sha'Tanya could get over the excitement of these new signups, Richelle, the most popular of the group, entered the classroom with ten additional students.

Sha'Tanya was ecstatic, as twenty students had bought into the pool in total, providing forty dollars, for a thirty-six-dollar jackpot. Sha'Tanya would receive a ten percent commission, allowing her to end the day with a twenty-seven-dollar earning, for a total of fifty-six dollars cash in hand.

Before Sha'Tanya could really savour this triumph, Akanni came running into the classroom, shouting excitedly.

"A fight's about to start next to the canteen," cried Akanni, doing a little dance, "two fifth formers fighting over a girl named Lystra!"

As all the students ran through the classroom door, onto the balcony, Sha'Tanya and Adrian briefly stared at each other with wide eyes. Up until the previous term, Lystra had been a long-standing friend of Sha'Tanya's, and since Sha'Tanya was really supposed to be in fifth form, she most likely knew the boys who were fighting over her. Sha'Tanya was briefly haunted by fond memories of times she'd spent with Lystra and her former best friend, Laurel. Those days were now behind her, but nevertheless, she had to see what was going on. She stuffed the newly received money into her bag pocket and zipped it up before jumping up with Adrian, to join the others.

In short order, a loud roar erupted from the student body and Sha'Tanya and Adrian were on the balcony, overlooking the canteen, observing a major fight. The fight was eventually broken up by a tall, slender, clear-skinned man, with an Adam's apple like a golf ball, and a hairline receding like a salary after taxes—Principal Wilberforce Harding. The spectators quickly dispersed, lamenting, as the principal led the boys away towards the main office.

"What the bird. I can't believe he carried the boys to the office," started Sha'Tanya, as she and Adrian made their way back inside the class. "I was there waiting to see Shane and Carlos get flogged."

Suddenly, Sha'Tanya stopped in her tracks, and gripped Adrian firmly by the wrist, stopping him as well.

"What?" asked Adrian, in a quizzical tone.

Sha'Tanya didn't render a response; she was rendered mute at the sight of an unzipped compartment of her backpack. She released Adrian's wrist and made a prompt investigation of the compartment, confirming her worst fear.

"All of my money ... gone," she whispered, with trembling hands, as she subtly surveyed the room. "Error."

"How?" whispered Adrian. "I thought you had a padlock."

"A lot of money was coming in," she whispered, pulling the padlock out of her pocket and starting to panic inside, "and then the fight happened; I ain't remember to lock the bag pocket."

"I told you this was a bad idea," Adrian muttered, as he performed a facepalm.

By this time, panic had fully overtaken Sha'Tanya, as the reality of her situation hit her like a bus named *Turbulence*. Mrs. Gibbs-Sealy would arrive after the second of two soundings of the school bell, and the results of the assignment would be known; she had to retrieve the money before the end of lunch, or explain to twenty angry children where the jackpot money was.

"I need to figure out who the culprit is," whispered Sha'Tanya, continuing to subtly scan the room as fire burned in her stomach, "as soon as possible."

"A lot of people were in here just before the fight started," whispered Adrian, in a sceptical tone, "any of them would have had opportunity."

"But all of them didn't know where I was keeping the money," Sha'Tanya replied, with a ponderous look, "only people that hired me this week, and the original people that joined the pool."

"It's Akanni; he was the first person that hired you," whispered Adrian, promptly, as he folded his arms. "That fat-lipped fool can't be trusted; he double-crossed me up to yesterday. He has intent—by character."

"It can't be Jerome; he's swimming in money already," Sha'Tanya pondered, verbally, while holding her chin, "and Kerrie seems to be a nice, soft girl—hates to get in trouble."

"I told you it is Akanni," whispered Adrian, intently, "he was the only one angry about the pool. Think back to how he stormed out earlier, vexed because you started a pool; that's motive right there."

"Allain was my first canteen customer, and the first person to join the pool," Sha'Tanya continued, ignoring Adrian for the moment, "he's a supporter, but he paused and gave me a strange look before agreeing to the pool; I don't think he was a hundred percent onboard with my commission."

"It … is … Akanni," said Adrian, through gnashed teeth, with agitated body language, "he's the one that called everybody out of the classroom, giving him ample opportunity to steal the money while we were busy watching the fight—intent, motive and opportunity!"

"It ain't Akanni," Sha'Tanya replied, with narrowed eyes, acknowledging Adrian's hypothesis for the first time, "it's Richelle."

"Really?" cried Adrian, before gathering himself and returning to a whisper. "Richelle has done nothing but sing your praises, and she's the one that brought the most people to join the pool."

"Yeah, she called me a smart girl, and said she gotta pay attention to me," said Sha'Tanya, rising from her seat, and scanning the room for Richelle, "but it ain't what people say, it's how they say it."

"I just laid out a perfectly logical case for Akanni's guilt," said Adrian, in an annoyed tone, jumping up from his seat, "and you're basing your findings on a feeling?"

"You may be better at reading books and facts, but I know how to read people, especially other girls," Sha'Tanya replied, firmly, pointing a finger at Adrian, "that girl was jealous of me, and I gotta find where she is and get back that money before the bell rings—follow me!"

Sha'Tanya dashed out of the classroom, with Adrian in hot pursuit.

"So, let's say you find her, what's to make her give it back?" started Adrian, trying to keep up with Sha'Tanya as she barrelled towards the stairs. "It's against the school rules to gamble; it's not like you can threaten to tell the principal."

Sha'Tanya paused at the bottom of the staircase, pondering Adrian's question.

"I can't threaten to tell Mr. Harding," said Sha'Tanya, staring at Adrian with one arm akimbo, "but I can threaten to beat it out of her!"

"Oh, that's realistic," cried Adrian, in a sarcastic tone, "I've known you for one year and I know you couldn't fight a mannequin!"

Sha'Tanya gave Adrian a look straight from hell.

"Just saying," cried Adrian, promptly, with his hands raised in a defensive posture, "at the first sign of physical trouble, you either find someplace to hide, or run the opposite direction!"

"I've never had to fight," cried Sha'Tanya, passionately, "I always had Laurel—from primary school!"

Sha'Tanya paused, and pondered for a moment, as Adrian looked on.

"That's it," she said, finally, with a grin, "I need Laurel."

"The same Laurel that disowned you?" cried Adrian. "I need to come up with another plan because that ain't likely to happen."

"If I can get children I barely know to give me over eighty dollars in three days, I gotta be able to get Laurel to frighten this girl for me," said Sha'Tanya, gripping Adrian by his shoulders and making direct eye contact. "Meet me outside the bathroom; Richelle should go to freshen up before the next period."

Sha'Tanya ran off with fire in her stomach. This was a make-or-break moment for her; if she couldn't get Laurel on board, she would have to confront Richelle on her own and that was not likely to go well for her. She knew she had uncovered an unexpected talent for negotiation, but Laurel had written her off completely, and she feared that it would take more persuasive powers than she possessed, to get Laurel to even consider helping her. Either way, she would soon find out, as she was on course for Laurel's usual hangout spot.

Several minutes later, Sha'Tanya was approaching Adrian, outside the bathroom—and she was alone.

"Richelle just went into the bathroom," cried Adrian, with folded arms. "It's a good thing I came up with another plan; I knew you couldn't get Laurel!"

"Don't talk to me right now," replied Sha'Tanya, pointing her index finger at Adrian, with fire in her eyes, "and I don't need your plan; I can deal with my own mess!"

She then proceeded to charge into the bathroom, leaving Adrian with a dropped jaw. Moments later, she was in the off-white bathroom, standing behind Richelle, who was fixing herself in front of a big mirror, set over a counter with sinks.

"If you want to partner with me, come and talk business," started Sha'Tanya, arms akimbo, looking at Richelle via her reflection in the mirror, "but don't be smiling in my face and stealing my money!"

Richelle turned around, promptly, with wide eyes.

"Don't be opening your eyes so wide at me," cried Sha'Tanya, sticking her chest out, "I know you took up my money!"

"You're smarter than people give you credit for," said Richelle, with a wide smile, "but you should be smart enough to know you can't do a thing 'bout it!"

"I know you ain't want to tango with Laurel," said Sha'Tanya, folding her arms, "so just return my money, and things ain't gotta get ugly!"

"You mean that big girl in fifth form?" Richelle replied, with a hearty laugh. "She ain't talking to you; who you trying to fool?"

"You willing to take that gamble?" asked Sha'Tanya, stepping forward to come face to face with Richelle, while her heart raced and anxiety burned within her stomach.

"Get out of my face, girl!" shouted Richelle, in a violent tone.

"Give me what belongs to me!" cried Sha'Tanya,

defiantly, trying not to show her fear of a physical confrontation. Her choice of words was probably ill-advised, as Richelle pushed her backwards and swiftly delivered a thundering slap to her face, sending her stumbling backwards even farther.

"This girl using lotion or cement on her skin?" thought Sha'Tanya, as she tried to regain her stability. "How on earth one hand could hit so hard?"

Finally, regaining her stability, Sha'Tanya stepped forward towards Richelle again; she was out of her depth but failure wasn't an option. Richelle lunged forward, gripping Sha'Tanya's shoulders with both hands, with her thumbs pressing into Sha'Tanya's neck. Before Sha'Tanya could respond properly, she was being pushed farther into the bathroom, past the sinks and into an area with toilet stalls. As Sha'Tanya tried to establish her own grip on Richelle, she felt herself being pushed into a stall door, which gave way, allowing her to be pushed into the stall itself. In short order, her feet were obstructed by a toilet, but Richelle's pushing did not abate, causing Sha'Tanya to stumble and fall backwards onto the toilet. She now had limited mobility, in the cramped stall, with her back against a toilet tank and Richelle's weight pressing down on her. She couldn't kick her attacker, and her hands seemed useless to her cause in that moment.

"This was a fatal error," she thought, as Richelle pinned her leg to the toilet seat with one knee, released one of her hands and raised it in a fist to smite her. "I can't believe this is the outcome of my work over the last three days."

Suddenly, a hand gripped Richelle by the neck and violently extracted her from the stall. Sha'Tanya looked up to see Richelle cowering before a big, thick, dark girl, with cornrows—Laurel.

"Girl, I would hit you so hard you would need plastic surgery to remove my hand print!" shouted Laurel, creating an echo in the bathroom. A shudder shot through Sha'Tanya, despite not being the one to whom Laurel's words were addressed; Laurel was known to be remarkably strong and she could only imagine what Richelle must have been feeling in that moment.

Sha'Tanya finally managed to lift herself from the toilet and exited the stall in time to see a trembling Richelle surrendering the money to Laurel.

"Count it!" cried Laurel, firmly, as she gave a stack of bills and loose coins to Sha'Tanya.

Sha'Tanya promptly obeyed, then gave Laurel a nod, indicating that all the money was accounted for. Laurel then pointed to the bathroom exit, prompting Richelle to evacuate the bathroom like her life depended on it.

"Girl, I ain't know what changed your mind," started Sha'Tanya, "but thank you so much; I ain't know what would have happened …"

"Don't thank me; I only came because my family really needs the money," interrupted Laurel, aggressively. "Give me what you promised me, or start looking for a good plastic surgeon!"

Sha'Tanya held her head down, with water settling in her eyes, and surrendered fifty-six dollars to Laurel, leaving her with only the thirty-six dollars she needed to pay the winner of the pool. Her tearfulness was not ushered in by the loss of money, however, but by the continued loss of a once great friendship.

"What were you even doing with all of this money?" asked Laurel as she took the funds from Sha'Tanya.

"I was saving up to pay for some extra lessons," Sha'Tanya replied, in a low voice, "I can't afford to fail this year again."

Laurel sighed, and then returned the fifty-six dollars to Sha'Tanya.

"Keep out of trouble," cried Laurel, intently, as she marched out of the bathroom, "and don't contact me again!"

Sha'Tanya stood for a moment, staring at the money in her hand, before drying her eyes and running out of the bathroom after Laurel.

"Laurel," she cried, catching up to her just outside the bathroom, as Adrian looked on in the near distance, "a deal is a deal; take the money!"

"Huh?" said Laurel, with a discombobulated look, as Sha'Tanya held out the money towards her, and Adrian approached their position.

"Truth is, you were always a better friend to me than I was to you," said Sha'Tanya, in a humble tone, as Adrian arrived, "you deserve it, and I know your family probably needs it more than me."

"Focusing on school work and putting other people before yourself?" cried Laurel, with shock etched upon her face. "You can't be Sha'Tanya Carter!"

"I couldn't believe it either," said Adrian, with his hands raised in a defensive posture, "I thought she was from an alternate universe."

"Who would have thought?" said Laurel, shaking her head as she took the money from Sha'Tanya, and the school bell rang.

As Laurel walked away, she stopped, looked back at Sha'Tanya and said, "I'll call you."

Sha'Tanya was emotionally stirred as she watched Laurel walk away. She had lost all her earnings, but she had managed to save herself from the wrath of her peers, and most importantly, she had regained a friend.

"Seems I owe you an apology; you are, indeed, dynamite," said Adrian, excitedly. "I want details and I want them now; fill me in!"

Sha'Tanya updated Adrian on their way to the classroom. Minutes later, the bell sounded for a second time, and Mrs. Gibbs-Sealy arrived for class with the results of the homework assignment. Akanni did, in fact, receive zero, allowing Jerome to win the pool, much to the dissatisfaction of the other children, who vowed never to participate in another pool.

Later that day, during an unexpected free period, Adrian asked Sha'Tanya about the future of her business schemes.

"So, is this the end of 'Sha'Tanya Enterprises'?" he asked, turning his head to look across at her from his desk.

"Error," replied Sha'Tanya, turning her body to make direct eye contact with Adrian, "I gotta build back my funds for lessons, but I need you to be my CCSO."

"Your what?" asked Adrian, with a look of utter discombobulation.

SHA'TANYA ENTERPRISES

"My chief common-sense officer," said Sha'Tanya, in an earnest tone. "If you see me making another questionable business decision … slap me!"

THE RECESSION OF WILBERFORCE HARDING

The heavy roar of a diesel engine pierced the quiet of an early morning, as a bus barrelled around a corner with a reckless lean. It glistened brightly in the morning sun, and was dressed with spoilers, roof racks and other accessories. Etched in its blue, decorative window tint was the name *Turbulence*, and loud music blasted out of it.

The bus came to a quick halt, just outside the front gate of a school and a multitude of children disembarked in a disorderly fashion. As they pushed and squeezed through the door, and jumped through windows of the bus, Sha'Tanya sat in the back seat, calmly observing the ensuing mayhem. Her peers were all rushing to get into the school before the bell rang, but Sha'Tanya wasn't worried about being a little tardy. After the mob subsided, Sha'Tanya exited with her excessively gelled hair glistening in the morning sunlight.

She casually made her way into the school, walking up a worn driveway, past the main office and up a long walkway set under a trellis. Waiting for her at the end of the trellis was a slim, dark boy, of average height, with folded arms and a stern look. This was her friend, Adrian; after an ill-fated, one-off disaster of a date two years prior, he had unexpectedly become one of her only friends.

"So, you show up early for school the whole term to study," started Adrian, sternly, as Sha'Tanya approached him at the end of the trellis, "and now that we are in full-blown promotion exam mode, you decide to slack off on the hype bus?"

"Be cool, I ain't repeating this year again; between extra lessons and help from you, I got this," replied Sha'Tanya, in an unflustered tone. "Besides, after all that hard work, I think I need a little excitement to keep things balanced."

"One of these days, that excitement is going to be your undoing, but it's a good sign that you are so confident of passing," said Adrian, relaxing his posture and tone, "it means I'm a great tutor."

"You should teach aerobics; you like to stretch things a bit too much," cried Sha'Tanya, with a scornful look on her face, "it was eighty percent lessons, and twenty percent help from you."

Suddenly, the school bell sounded, and Sha'Tanya started to walk away towards the school hall, in the near distance.

"Hey, not so fast," Adrian cried, as he moved to catch up to her, "I'd say it was more sixty percent lessons, and forty percent Adrian!"

"We gotta get to assembly," said Sha'Tanya, dismissively, as she entered the hall, receiving a grunt from Adrian in reply.

It wasn't long before the hall filled with children and a short, stocky, spectacled teacher mounted the platform.

"Oh no; Mrs. Gibbs-Sealy on the 'flatform'," Sha'Tanya said to Adrian, who was standing next to her. "I can't believe they sent the most long-winded teacher in the school to do assembly; by the end of this I might be in a coma."

"Diurnal salutations to this fine, formative assemblage," started Mrs. Gibbs-Sealy, in a shrill, enthusiastic voice.

Sha'Tanya didn't understand a word of what Mrs. Gibbs-Sealy had said, neither did she care; she slipped into her own mental world and didn't hear another word until assembly was coming to an end. At that time, the long-winded English teacher gave way to the tall, dark guidance councillor, Mrs. Gill, who had some announcements to make.

"Firstly, I would like to officially announce the retirement of Mr. Peters when this term concludes shortly," said Mrs. Gill, as a tall, slim, greying man crossed the platform and took a bow.

Sha'Tanya bumped fists with Adrian as the children applauded Mr. Peters' retirement; at the beginning of that school year, Adrian had petitioned Principal Harding to replace Mr. Peters, who had a history of dropping to sleep in classes.

"It's about time," Sha'Tanya whispered to Adrian, as the applause subsided. "He passed his expiry date a long time ago."

"Secondly," started Mrs. Gill, as a thick, dark, rough-looking man with grey stubble trotted across the platform, "Principal Harding is on an indefinite personal leave; in his absence, Mr. Greenidge is the acting principal."

Mr. Greenidge was a history teacher who had recently become the deputy principal. Sha'Tanya knew him to be a little rough around the edges, but she considered him a cool teacher, and was intrigued by his sudden promotion.

"This should be interesting," Sha'Tanya whispered to Adrian with a smile, as Mr. Greenidge took over from Mrs. Gill. "This should be a fun end-of-year!"

That assertion would soon be shattered, as Mr. Greenidge proceeded to outline immediate changes.

"Effective immediately, the pass mark for students repeating a year will be ten percent higher," said Mr. Greenidge, "this is a school, not a hotel; if you can't ace the work the second time around, this isn't the place for you."

"Error," whispered Sha'Tanya, as her stomach lit up like a furnace.

"Also," continued Mr. Greenidge, "there is a zero-tolerance policy on tardiness and absenteeism; anyone not at assembly when the bell rings will be flogged!"

"Double error," whispered Sha'Tanya, as the hall collectively gasped.

"And in case anyone thinks that this is a hollow threat," started Mr. Greenidge, "send in the children, Mrs. Gibbs-Sealy, and bring me *The Nemesis*!"

Sha'Tanya looked on in horror and disbelief, as

six children from across the school were led across the platform by Mrs. Gibbs-Sealy, who was holding a massive piece of bamboo. Mrs. Gibbs-Sealy delivered the bamboo to Mr. Greenidge like a sceptre being given to a king, and he proceeded to acquaint the posteriors of the children with *The Nemesis*.

As the floggings occurred, Sha'Tanya could hear her peers struggling to suppress their snickers, but she did not find the floggings funny at all. As someone who had a history of tardiness, the sound of every lash and every whimper pierced her to the core; it could very well be her on that platform being humiliated in front of the entire school.

Finally, the floggings concluded and assembly came to an end with a chilling warning.

"To those of you who get to school late, and those of you who like to skip assembly—you will be found," said Mr. Greenidge, forcefully. "Girls, I will be sounding my voice and entering bathrooms; no one is safe—dismissed!"

Assembly had ended, but Mr. Greenidge's announcements marred the entire day. Losing Principal Harding wasn't such a great thing after all. Everyone was on edge, and Sha'Tanya wasn't feeling as confident as she did before. She was doing her fourth year for the second time, which now meant that she would be held to a higher standard in her promotion exams.

The next morning, Sha'Tanya was standing in the bus yard, waiting on a bus to go to school. As she stood on a sidewalk, looking at the buses before her in a big paved area, she heard a familiar voice calling her.

"Sha'Tanya!" cried a male voice. "Fancy meeting you here this fine Friday."

She looked in the direction of the voice to see Adrian approaching her position. She didn't usually see him on mornings as he caught the bus from the bus yard, whereas she usually walked up to the hospital to get the bus before it reached the yard. That was the best way to ensure she got a seat, but that morning was different.

"You look like you got hit by *Turbulence*," said Adrian, with a chuckle. "What cat dragged you into the bus yard?"

"I ain't in the mood for your smart remarks," replied Sha' Tanya, giving Adrian a deadpan stare, "I had a hard night studying, got up too late to catch *Turbulence* on the early trip, and ain't got the energy to walk up by the 'horsepital' now—nor to dodge the truancy officer."

"I thought you were confident of passing your exams," started Adrian, folding his arms. "I wanted you to take the exams seriously but don't let Mr. Greenidge get under your skin."

"That's easy for you to say," cried Sha'Tanya, with one arm akimbo, "he's holding a scholar like you to a lower standard than somebody like me that needs extra lessons!"

"Relax; you got this," said Adrian, relaxing his posture.

"I ain't so sure 'bout that," she replied, with a little less attitude, "I might gotta look into this cheating ring I was hearing 'bout."

"Cheating is beneath you," said Adrian, with

a scornful look. "I've worked with you; you're good enough to pass—easily."

Sha'Tanya gave Adrian a sceptical look. She wished she could be as confident in herself as he seemed to be, but there was too much at stake for her to be at peace.

"It's interesting; this is the exact spot where I first met you properly—where I first learned your name," started Adrian, as if in prophetic reply to her thoughts. "You were so determined, confident and sure of yourself back then, I saw you as an African goddess; apply that confidence to your school work."

"You really saw me as an African goddess?" asked Sha'Tanya, blushing.

"That wasn't the point I was making … actually, forget I said that," Adrian replied, with his hands up in a defensive posture. "Just believe in yourself; when you're determined and confident in yourself, you seem to be able to accomplish anything."

At that moment, a bus came into the yard and stopped in the near distance for passengers to disembark.

"Come," said Adrian, "let's get to school before we get flogged on the platform."

"I really want to get to school early, but I don't think I can bring myself to get in this plain, old, rust-bucket bus," Sha'Tanya thought, before expressing the thought in a single word.

"Error!"

"I know, I know; you can't be seen in a plain, rust-bucket bus," said Adrian, as he walked away from her position towards the bus. "I just hope I don't see you paraded across the platform to meet *The Nemesis*!"

"Double error!" she shouted, with a snarky attitude, but deep down inside, she hoped she wasn't making a critical mistake.

As time rolled on, Sha'Tanya became more and more nervous about her decision to wait on a favourable bus. Adrian's bus had long gone, and several buses travelling to South Sea Village had come and gone, with no sign of *Turbulence*, nor her backup bus, *The Road Warrior*.

Finally, after what seemed like forever, she heard a familiar rumble and knew that *Turbulence* was on its way into the yard. She started to move towards the position she knew it would stop, and readied herself to battle the multitude of children who were also waiting to board it. In short order, the bus came barrelling into the yard and scores of children rushed upon it like ants attacking a sweet treat.

"South Sea with seats and moving!" cried the clear, tall, lanky conductor as he jumped through the door and moved out of the path of the ants.

The fight was brutal as the incoming ants clashed with the disembarking passengers. There were children already inside the bus, who had boarded before it reached the yard and some children were climbing through windows; the chances of Sha'Tanya getting a seat were infinitesimal at best—and she knew it. When she finally managed to propel herself through the door, she headed straight for the engine.

The engine was positioned at the front of the bus, between the driver and a single seat for the front passenger, and its cover featured an airbrushed painting of a plane flying through a lightning-filled, dark blue sky. It was also used as an area for bags to be heaped and as a seat for only the most popular children who failed to secure a regular seat. Sha'Tanya had much history with that bus and its crew, so she proudly took her seat on the engine cover. Centimetres away from her, in the driver seat, was "Count Dracula", also known simply as "The Count". He was a tall, highly clear-skinned man with the sides of his head shaved and long plaits falling from the top of his head. In his mouth were monstrous looking teeth, in desperate need of dental work—hence the name, Count Dracula.

As children continued to stream into the bus and fight for seats, Sha'Tanya heard another familiar engine, and a musical air horn, followed by much commotion from outside and inside of her bus.

"Men, *Road Warrior* now land in the yard!" came an excited cry from the back of the bus.

Sha'Tanya tingled with excitement as the atmosphere inside the bus became more hype and children from a neighbouring school, South Sea Secondary, descended upon *The Road Warrior*, which was their ride of choice. The mood suddenly became competitive in her bus, with the children calling for a race.

"This was worth it," thought Sha'Tanya, as both buses revved their engines to depart, "I get to experience the race of the year, and with the speeds these buses about to hit, I should get to school before the bell."

Her excitement shot through the roof as the driver

put on loud music, revved the engine and shot out of the yard with the other bus in hot pursuit. What followed was a wild, rapid, reckless ride, with both buses rocking from side to side and reaching dangerous speeds when traffic permitted.

Halfway into her journey, Sha'Tanya's excitement turned into apprehension, as she spotted a police officer on a motorcycle, in the line of oncoming traffic.

"Count," she cried, alerting the driver next to her, "'motorbycle' cop in the traffic!"

"Respect, Sha'Tanya!" replied The Count, as he suddenly careened the bus off the main road and through a minor road on the left.

As the bus completed the turn, Sha,Tanya looked through the front passenger window, into the rear view mirror to catch a glimpse of *The Road Warrior* turning into the minor road behind them. Under normal circumstances, Sha'Tanya would have found much excitement in being driven off the designated route, but on this occasion, the fires of anxiety burned within her stomach like magma bubbling in a volcano before an eruption.

"I can't be put off this bus," she thought, earnestly hoping that the police officer hadn't seen them, as The Count sped along the minor road.

Her hopes were shattered in short order by the piercing sound of a police siren.

"People 'bout the island doing real crimes and these 'motorbycle' cops out here hunting down buses," thought Sha'Tanya, as The Count brought the bus to a stop and the bike rode past it, with *The Road Warrior* stopped behind.

THE RECESSION OF WILBERFORCE HARDING

As the officer dismounted the bike in front of *Turbulence* to report both buses, Sha'Tanya's thought was verbalised in a single word.

"Error!" she cried, as she gripped her backpack and rose from the engine, in preparation for her impending expulsion.

"Alright, don't waste my time," cried the big, incredibly dark officer with huge ears, "I want only seven standing passengers, counting from the back, and one passenger per seat!"

Sha'Tanya wasted no time in disembarking the bus; she was familiar with the process, so she knew it was coming. She also knew that she had to move quickly if she had any desire to reboard the bus. Fortunately, she had been taken off-route in that area many times before, and she knew exactly where she had to run.

As the officer's attention was on removing children from the bus, she slipped through a narrow residential street and started to run. A few children followed her, and though she could hear their footsteps behind her, her focus was not on them; she knew she had to reach a particular point on the main road before the bus passed there.

"Lord, if this is punishment for selling out my cousin to the police, have mercy," she prayed in her mind as she ran through a battered street, between middleclass houses, "I need to get back in that bus and get to school before the bell; deliver me from the evil that is *The Nemesis*."

Minutes later, she was running through another street and she could see the main road in the near distance. Her feet were hurting and her backpack felt like two oxygen tanks on her back, but she heard the engine of the bus and mustered the fortitude to push her feet harder.

In short order, the bus appeared and Sha'Tanya started to wave and shout, barely managing to catch the driver's eye.

"You gotta make it quick," shouted The Count, as he stopped the bus, prompting Sha'Tanya to run like she had never run before, "I ain't want to be here picking up children when that officer finish reporting the other bus!"

A group of her peers were running behind her but Sha'Tanya, who had a head start by exiting the bus promptly, reached the bus first. She rushed around the bus and sprang through the door as The Count revved the engine and shot off. She took her seat on the engine cover just in time to see her peers being left behind, through the driver's window.

For the remainder of the trip, Sha'Tanya was in a pensive mood, sobered by the realisation that she could have been one of the unfortunate children left behind. Excitement became irrelevant to her; she just wanted to make it to school before the bell.

Finally, the bus approached the school, and Sha'Tanya went into a panic as she looked through the windscreen.

"No, I can't be seeing right," she thought, as she processed the sight before her eyes, "this 'windscream' gotta be playing tricks on my eyes."

As the bus came to a stop in front of the school

gate, she got an instant headache as panic shot through her heart like an arrow. Right outside the gate was Mr. Greenidge, and he wasn't alone; *The Nemesis* was with him. Sha'Tanya didn't know if the floggings would transpire at the gate or in the hall, and she didn't care to find out—but what could she do? What could any of the children do but disembark the bus and face the chilling music?

In a few minutes, the children had disembarked and were about to be escorted into the school by the acting principal, when the highly accessorised *Road Warrior* passed and recklessly swerved off a stationary *Turbulence*, en route to South Sea Secondary.

With the seats and aisle empty, The Count revved the engine and shot off behind his competitor, leaving the poor children to face *The Nemesis* and its wielder. As he sped away from the school gate, Sha'Tanya ascended from a crouch, between two seats, and addressed the driver.

"Put me off 'round the corner, Count," she shouted, raising her voice above the music which had been significantly lowered since the children had disembarked, "I gotta get in this school another way!"

"What the bird," cried the conductor, "you ain't easy, Sha'Tanya!"

"You gotta bail, sweet girl," cried The Count, "I' trying to get in South Sea Village to clean up any passengers going to town before *Road Warrior*!"

"Easy!" cried Sha'Tanya, as she confidently made her way to the door.

As the bus turned the corner, The Count reduced

speed just enough for Sha'Tanya to jump through the door and hit the ground in stride, before shooting off up the road. Sha'Tanya skilfully maintained her balance, gradually decreasing speed until she could safely stop.

As the bus sped off in the distance, Sha'Tanya's attention turned to the tall wall of the school, which she now stood beside. She ran to a particular section of the wall, which was much lower but still somewhat high. In short order, she was pulling herself over the top of the wall, and carefully descending the other side, until she was safely standing in a concreted area at the back of the school. The area was deserted, featuring a seldom used water tank, a full garbage skip which was cleared at the end of each week, and a small building which housed the school kiln. The kiln had been inoperative for a long time, but earlier that year, Adrian had managed to convince Principal Harding to fix it. Still, it was not a frequently used building, making this the perfect point of entry for Sha'Tanya.

"I can't believe I just climbed that wall with this backpack," Sha'Tanya thought, recounting past times she had considered and rejected such a climb.

Her headache had now subsided but before she could settle herself, she heard heavy footsteps approaching and started to look around franticly for a place of concealment. In seconds, a big, tall, clear-skinned guard entered the area and looked around. A few seconds later, he left, leaving Sha'Tanya to breathe a sigh of relief from a very tight hideout between the garbage skip and the wall. Despite the guard's departure, she remained in her smelly, tight position, until she heard children nearby, signalling the end of assembly.

Satisfied that assembly had ended, she made her way into the body of the school, and set a course for her classroom, relieved that her ordeal was over. She assured herself that she could make it through the few remaining weeks of the school year; she just had to wake up early every morning, and find a sure way of passing her promotion exams, despite the higher bar set for her.

In short order, she was ascending a narrow staircase, and dashing into her classroom. As soon as she entered, Adrian sprang up from his seat at the second of six desks, in the first of four rows, and tried to address her, but she had no time for him.

"Not now, Adrian," she cried, dashing past him, "I' on a mission!"

In seconds, she was standing before a bony, pale white boy, resembling a whitewashed stick insect, who sat in the middle of the classroom. This was Jerome Atkins, a filthy-rich boy, who was prone to academic failure.

"There's supposed to be a cheating ring in the school," she said, leaning on Jerome's desk and making direct eye contact with him, "I want in."

"You think I have something to do with a cheating ring?" Jerome asked, with a little laugh.

"If anybody stands to benefit from cheating, it's you!" replied Sha'Tanya, emphatically. "No offense, but you' got more zeros than a chequebook!"

"No offense taken; that was funny," cried Jerome, with another laugh. "You may be right but I have no time for cheating; I pay for my promotions. You could try Akanni."

Before Sha'Tanya could pursue further inquiries, she felt a hand tapping her back, and turned around promptly to see Adrian.

"I know, I know … you want to know what happened this morning," she started, with one arm akimbo, "I climbed over the wall, but I ain't got time right now to go into …"

"Forget that," Adrian interrupted, "at the end of assembly, Mr. Greenidge flogged a whole set of children that arrived late, on *Turbulence*—then banned the school!"

"Huh?" Sha'Tanya exclaimed, with a confounded look. "Banned the school from what?"

"Effective next week, anybody caught on *Turbulence* or *The Road Warrior* will be suspended from school!" cried Adrian, with wide eyes.

"Error!" screamed Sha'Tanya, her voice echoing through the class, commanding the attention of every student as she stared at Adrian with wide eyes.

At that moment, a short, stout, dark, male teacher with a bald patch entered the classroom, and made his way to the big teacher's desk at the front of the room, ending the conversation. Adrian returned to his seat, and Sha'Tanya took up her position next to him, at the first desk in the first row.

The conversation might have ended but it continued to reverberate through Sha'Tanya's mind. Not long ago, she had assured herself that she could make it through the few remaining weeks of the school year, but now, she was sure she couldn't. Mr. Greenidge had to go, and the only way to accomplish that was to bring Principal Wilberforce Harding out of his recession.

By the next day, which was a Saturday, Sha'Tanya had come up with a plan, and she wasted no time in setting that plan in motion. By midday, she was in a remote part of the country, walking along a worn road with more holes than a colander, in a short denim pants, a short, white shirt and a pair of white brand-name sneakers. Her shiny hair was rendered motionless by the usual abundance of hair gel, and her neck was powdered. Next to her was a grumpy Adrian, in a red t-shirt, long blue jeans and a pair of white sneakers.

"I can't believe I let you talk me into this," Adrian grumbled, as he threaded the worn road set between bushes, "this ain't necessary; you could have called!"

"Error," cried Sha'Tanya, holding up one hand in a defensive posture, "that ain't personal enough; a phone can't carry the emotional weight I need today!"

"You seem to have this all figured out and under control," Adrian grumbled, "I don't need to be here!"

"Double error," cried Sha'Tanya, emphatically, as they approached a secluded, walled property, "I need you for backup; you have a history of convincing this man to do things!"

"I wouldn't go that far," murmured Adrian.

"You got this man to fix the kiln, replace a P.E. teacher and send Mr. Peters into retirement," cried Sha'Tanya, with arms akimbo, as the pair reached the walled property, "so don't try to downplay your skills!"

Sha'Tanya led Adrian along the green guard wall, to a wide, grey, double-door gate.

"Just pray that this is the right property," she said, as she tried to find a doorbell.

"Well, it would sure be fitting," murmured Adrian, "it's recessed as far from the main road as his hairline is from his forehead."

"You are too much," cried Sha'Tanya, with a hearty laugh, as she ended her search for a doorbell, concluding there was none. "We gotta go over this wall!"

Seconds later, Sha'Tanya was springing over the top of the wall and landing in a big clay-tiled front yard, several metres away from a modest, mint-green, bricked bungalow. In short order, she heard Adrian landing next her, still grumbling.

"Bingo," cried Sha'Tanya, pointing to a grey SUV in the yard, which she recognised as belonging to Principal Harding, "we got the right house!"

"Hurray," said Adrian, in a lacklustre tone, as they started to move towards the house.

"I can't believe this is the great Adrian Manning, king of adventure, grumbling 'bout being on a big adventure," Sha'Tanya retorted, as they moved.

"Adventure Adrian is dead," said Adrian, emphatically, "we all have to evolve at some time—become our best selves."

Suddenly, Sha'Tanya's heartrate shot up as two big, black dogs came charging from behind the house, barking aggressively as they approached her position.

"Run for the SUV!" cried Adrian, as he grabbed her hand and started to run.

THE RECESSION OF WILBERFORCE HARDING

Sha'Tanya thought her heart would burst through her chest as she ran towards the vehicle, with the dogs rapidly gaining on them. Finally, she reached the vehicle and followed Adrian's lead, stepping on the big, right-side, front tyre to boost herself onto the bonnet, and then gripping one of the roof racks to pull herself up onto the roof of the vehicle.

Now, crouched on top of the vehicle with Adrian, Sha'Tanya gripped the roof rack and watched in horror as the dogs circled the vehicle, jumping up, trying to reach them.

"You see why Adventure Adrian is dead?" cried Adrian, in an agitated tone. "I'm way too valuable to continue putting myself in these dangerous situations!"

Sha'Tanya didn't respond; on this occasion she didn't have a snarky comeback for Adrian's comment. She just hoped for an intervention of some kind.

In that moment, her mind was flooded with questions, "Is anyone home? Is Mr. Harding incapacitated or in hospital? How can we possibly get out of this secluded yard without being mauled?"

To her relief, the front door of the house flew open, to reveal a tall, slender, clear-skinned man, with a colossal Adam's apple, and a hairline in greater recession than a shoreline with erosion—Principal Wilberforce Harding. He stepped out onto a small patio, grabbed two leashes and then charged into the yard, promptly securing the two dogs and leashing them to the gate.

"You trying to make me fully bald?" asked Mr. Harding, staring intently at the two teenagers, who had finally dismounted the SUV. "How did you even find this house?"

"The phonebook," replied Sha'Tanya, boldly, "I figured there couldn't be many mothers naming their babies Wilberforce—no offence."

"Normally, I would blame Mr. Manning for such a stunt, but you, Miss Carter, seem to be the mastermind this time," said Mr. Harding, with an intrigued look on his face, as both he and Adrian stared at Sha'Tanya. "Why are you on my property this bright Saturday afternoon?"

"Sir, the truth is that we never realised how much we really appreciated you, till somebody else took over the role," started Sha'Tanya, with an earnest quality. "We came to make sure you are okay, and to make sure you ain't thinking 'bout retiring before we graduate."

"Wow," said Mr. Harding, in a pensive tone, "I was not prepared for this at all; I never dreamed that students would go to these lengths to keep me around."

Sha'Tanya felt triumphant at the sound of those words. She had achieved the emotional weight she wanted from her gesture—but Mr. Harding wasn't done yet.

"I have a medical procedure on Monday, and based on the projected recovery time, I'll be out for the rest of the term," started Mr. Harding, assuming a relaxed posture.

"To be honest, I was thinking about retiring early, to preserve what little hair I have left," continued Mr. Harding, "but after what you've done here today, I'm going to make a deal with you; pass your promotion exams, and I will be back for your fifth form year!"

Sha'Tanya wasn't sure how to feel in that moment. She had succeeded in reaching Mr. Harding, both physically and emotionally, and she had done so without Adrian's assistance. However, this had not changed her immediate reality; she had still lost *Turbulence* for the rest of the term, she still had to meet a higher standard than her peers for her promotion exams, and now, if she failed, this would be her reality for the rest of her life at the school—if she wasn't kicked out. More than ever before, the cheating scheme seemed like the only logical path to salvation, but somehow, in that moment, she couldn't get Adrian's words out of her head.

"I saw you as an African goddess," she remembered him saying the day before in the bus yard, "just believe in yourself; when you're determined and confident in yourself, you seem to be able to accomplish anything."

"So, do we have a deal?" asked Mr. Harding, extending his hand towards her after a little pause on Sha'Tanya's end.

"Sure, we have a deal," replied Sha'Tanya, shaking his hand firmly, thinking that maybe, she might actually have been underrating herself.

A few weeks later, it was the last week of school, exams were completed and Sha'Tanya had been unexpectedly summoned to the principal's office. As she sat in the cold office, sandwiched between a big trophy cabinet and the principal's huge desk, she was inundated with apprehension; the last time she had been summoned to that office, it was to inform her that she would be denied promotion. Behind the desk, sat the rough-looking, grey-stubbled acting principal, Mr. Greenidge.

"I wanted you to hear it from me," said the acting principal, in a firm voice, "before you saw it on your end-of-year report."

Sha'Tanya's heart raced as she anxiously awaited the next line. The last person to utter those words to her was Mr. Harding, right before informing her that she would be repeating her fourth year.

"Since you were repeating a year, you needed to score ten percent over the regular pass mark," said Mr. Greenidge, giving her an intense stare. "Young lady, you scored twenty-five percent over the regular pass mark, the best score on your record to date; whatever you did this year, keep it up!"

Sha'Tanya was flooded with a bevy of emotions, from surprise, to joy, to pride. These emotions compromised the usually well-kept reservoir behind her eyes, resulting in a stream of tears.

For several weeks, she had fostered much resentment for Mr. Greenidge and his draconian measures, but in that moment, she actually found herself feeling grateful for all that had transpired. Though she wasn't quite ready to give up hype buses for good, through the challenges from Mr. Greenidge, Adrian and Mr. Harding, she had learned that she could survive without hype, and most importantly, she had learned never to underrate herself, for she had achieved the best grade of her life—without cheating.

Adrian's words echoed through her head in that

moment, "we all have to evolve at some time—become our best selves."

As she thanked Mr. Greenidge and rose to leave the office, she rose with a new confidence and a new determination. She knew it would be hard work, but as she pulled the door to leave the office, she silently told herself, "Graduation, here I come!"

Sha'Tanya
UNLIMITED

Barbadian school girl, Sha'Tanya Carter, has been through much upheaval and adversity, but she's finally ready to graduate secondary school and become her best self. The birth of her best self, however, requires the death of her worst self.

From her love of recklessness and hype buses, to her hair gel addiction, to the very roots of her ghetto socialisation, all things that limit her must be tried by fire.

Before Sha'Tanya can ascend to her true calling, she must survive encounters with criminals, police officers, vindictive rivals and death itself, as she faces peril like never before!

How will Sha'Tanya survive these perils? What will it take for her to become her best self? What does that version of Sha'Tanya even look like?

Find out in this epic conclusion, as the refining fires of life finally give rise to a new Sha'Tanya—unlimited!

Sha'Tanya also appears in the *Adrian* Series

www.marioherbert.com

Redcore
PUBLISHING

9 789769 559493